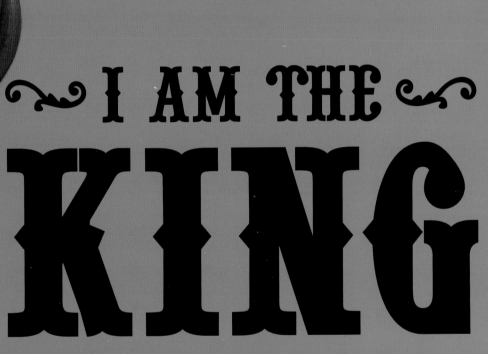

I AM THE KING

Written and Illustrated by
LEO TIMMERS

Clavis

NEW YORK

One morning, Turtle woke up and discovered
something new.
"Wow! There is a crown on my back!" he exclaimed.
"And it fits perfectly!"
Turtle toddled over to his friends and cried out,

"I AM THE KING!"

But his friends just laughed at him.

"You? The king?" Billy Goat chuckled. "That is impossible."

"Why?" Turtle asked.

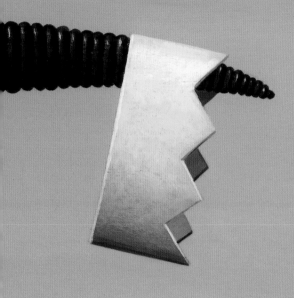

"Because you're way too slow, that's why,"
Billy Goat answered.
"A real king should have a long, white beard, just like me.
You see, the crown fits me perfectly."

"I AM THE KING!"

"Don't make me laugh," Flamingo said.
"You don't even have a real beard; it's a goatee.
Most of all, a king should be elegant.
This crown looks lovely on me."

"I AM THE KING!"

"You sssilly feather-head," Snake hissed.

"A king should be sssly like a sssnake.

Look, I can do sssomething ssspecial with thisss crown.

Don't you think it fitsss me fabulousssly?"

"I AM THE KING!"

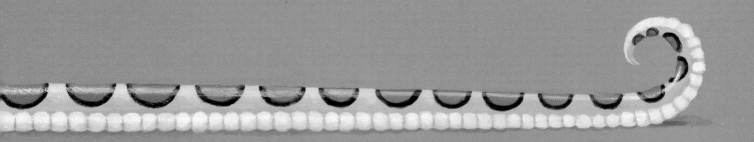

"Rubbish!" Pig proclaimed.
"A king should be pudgy.
I know just how to handle this crown.
Look, it's just my size."

"I AM THE KING!"

"Ridiculous!" Crocodile snapped.
"We have no use for a fat king.
We need someone tough.
Hand me that crown!
You see, it fits me perfectly."

"I AM THE KING!"

"Friends, listen up," Elephant exclaimed.

"Don't be upset, but none of you are suited to be king.

A king should be old and wise.

The crown only fits me perfectly.

Ah, I feel so very royal."

"I AM THE KING!"

"Woo hoo!" Ape screamed.

"A king plays funny tricks, like I do.

That crown is mine! See ya!"

And Ape ran off with the crown, shouting,

"I AM THE KING!"

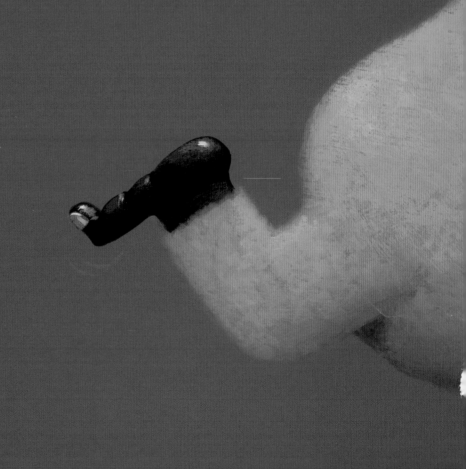

"Hold it, thief!" Elephant trumpeted.
"Why, if I ever catch you . . ." Crocodile snapped.
"Come back here!" Pig squealed.
"Ssstop!" Snake hissed.
"Give it back!" Flamingo squawked.
"It's my crown!" Billy Goat bleated.
"It's not fair!" Turtle whined.

Because Ape was running so fast, he tripped and fell and
bumped his head. Then everything was quiet. Very, very quiet.
"Lion," someone whispered.

Solemnly, without saying a word,
Lion picked up the crown and put it on his head.
"It fits perfectly!" Ape cried out with surprise.
"Yes!" they all exclaimed, and cheered in unison,

"LION IS THE KING!"
"LONG LIVE THE KING!"

I Am The King written and illustrated by Leo Timmers
Original title: Ik ben de koning
Translated from Dutch by Inge Van den Abeele-Kinget
Edited by Hannele Rubin

ISBN 978-1-60537-018-7

Manufactured in China
First Edition
10 9 8 7 6 5 4 3 2 1